The Haunting of Blackwood Hall

Dorian Cross

Published by sinister stories, 2024.

This is a work of fiction. Similarities to real people, places, or events are entirely coincidental.

THE HAUNTING OF BLACKWOOD HALL

First edition. July 26, 2024.

ISBN: 979-8227946683

Written by Dorian Cross.

Table of Contents

Introduction

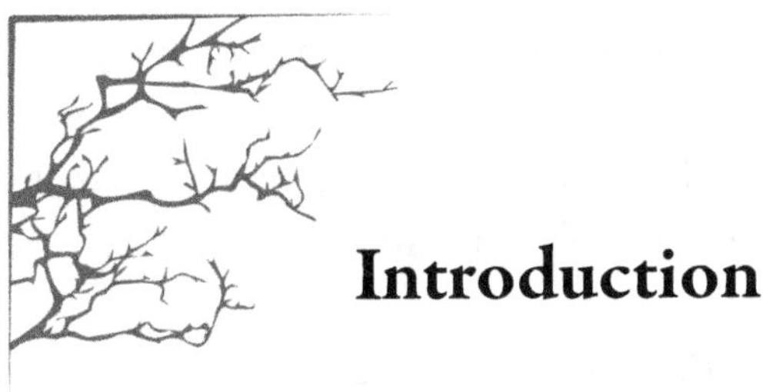

In the dim light of a stormy night, a mansion stands shrouded in mystery and shadow. Blackwood Hall, an imposing relic of a bygone era, has long been a subject of local legends and whispered tales. Its weathered walls and decaying grandeur tell a story of secrets buried deep within the fabric of its history. The manor's once-grand halls are now haunted by echoes of the past — whispers of long-forgotten sorrows and restless spirits seeking resolution.

For generations, Blackwood Hall has been more than just an old house; it has been a beacon for those drawn to the unknown. Its allure lies in the enigmatic past of the Blackwood family, whose name is synonymous with both power and tragedy. The manor's history is a tapestry woven with threads of occult practices, family feuds, and dark secrets that have remained hidden from the world.

Evelyn Harper, a dedicated historian with a passion for unraveling the mysteries of the past, finds herself at the heart of this enigma. Her journey begins with a seemingly ordinary investigation into the hall's dark history, but she soon discovers that it holds far more than just historical artifacts. It is a portal to a realm where the past is not so easily laid to rest.

As Evelyn delves deeper into the hall's secrets, she unearths a hidden legacy that connects the Blackwood family to ancient and powerful forces. The ghostly apparitions and eerie occurrences are not merely remnants of a bygone era but are intertwined with a broader and more sinister history. The hall becomes a stage where the echoes of the forgotten come alive, revealing the complex and often terrifying truths that have shaped its dark legacy.

In *The Haunting of Blackwood Hall*, the boundaries between the living and the dead blur as Evelyn Harper navigates a labyrinth of intrigue, danger, and the supernatural. Each chapter unravels another layer of the mystery, leading her — and the reader — further into a world where history and hauntings converge in unexpected and chilling ways.

Prepare yourself to step into the shadows of Blackwood Hall, where every corner holds a secret, every sound has a story, and the echoes of the past reverberate through the present. The adventure begins now, as the forgotten whispers rise to reveal their truths.

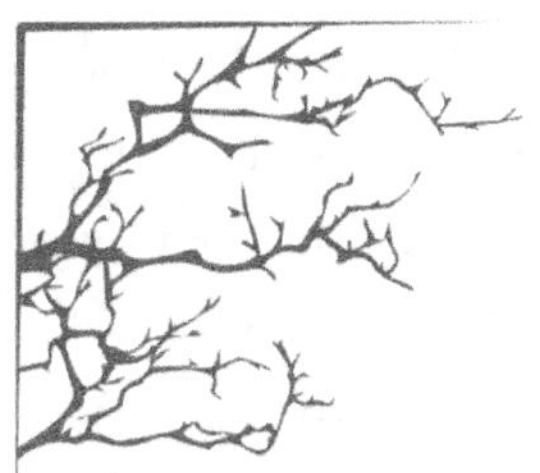

Chapter 1

The old-fashioned clock on the mantle struck midnight as a storm raged outside, rattling the windows of Blackwood Hall. The mansion, once grand and full of life, now stood silent and brooding in the heart of the sprawling countryside. Its towering spires and weathered stone façade seemed to absorb the fury of the tempest, creating an atmosphere of desolation.

Inside, Evelyn Harper's footsteps echoed through the empty halls as she made her way to the study. She was a historian, known for her work on restoring forgotten legacies and unearthing hidden histories. Tonight, however, she was here for a more personal reason. Her estranged uncle, Arthur Blackwood, had passed away, and she had inherited the mansion. The inheritance came with strings attached — if she wished to claim her property, she had to spend at least one night in the manor.

The air in the mansion was heavy with the scent of aged wood and mildew. Each step Evelyn took disturbed the dust that had settled over the years, sending tiny particles swirling in the dim light of her flashlight. The storm outside seemed to intensify, with thunder crashing and lightning illuminating the grand but neglected interior of the house. The once opulent furnishings were now draped in white sheets, their silhouettes ghostly in the flickering light.

As she approached the study, she couldn't shake the feeling of being watched. Her instincts told her it was merely the shadows and the creaking of the house settling under the weight of the storm. Yet, there was something more — a whisper in the wind, a chill that seemed to follow her as she walked.

She pushed open the study door, revealing a room filled with dust-covered books, old maps, and faded photographs. The study had been Arthur's sanctuary, and it was cluttered with the remnants of his obsession. His old desk, although covered in a thick layer of dust, had been recently disturbed. Papers were strewn about, as though someone had been searching for something.

Her gaze fell upon a large, open leather-bound journal on the desk. The pages were filled with a mix of handwritten notes and newspaper clippings. She hesitated before picking it up, feeling the weight of Arthur's intense focus in each word.

The journal was open, revealing a hastily scrawled entry:

"To whoever reads this: Beware. The shadows here hold more than just memories. There are things better left undisturbed. Arthur Blackwood."

Evelyn frowned, brushing off the dust and flipping through the pages. Arthur had been a reclusive man, obsessed with the mansion's dark history and the tales of ghosts that surrounded it. His obsession had led him to isolate himself from the world, and his journals were filled with cryptic notes and strange symbols. Some entries were almost frantic, describing events that seemed to defy logic.

A sudden gust of wind burst through the study's open window, sending papers flying and extinguishing the candlelight. Evelyn scrambled to close the window, her heart racing. The room was plunged into darkness, the only light coming from occasional flashes of lightning outside.

In the brief illumination, she saw a shadowy figure standing by the fireplace. Her breath caught in her throat as she stared at the apparition — a translucent form with an almost human shape but with features obscured by the darkness. The figure seemed to be reaching out towards her, its movement slow and deliberate.

She rubbed her eyes, convinced it was a trick of the light or a result of her fatigue. But the figure remained, its presence noticeable and unsettling. The apparition's mouth moved, forming silent words that Evelyn could not hear. Panic surged through her as she grabbed the nearest object — a heavy candlestick — and took a step forward. But before she could react, the figure vanished, leaving only the sound of the storm and the pounding of her own heart.

Determined to understand what she had seen, Evelyn turned her attention back to the desk. She carefully examined the scattered papers and old documents, looking for clues about the ghostly figure or the mansion's history. The journal's entries became increasingly erratic, mentioning the spirits of the manor and the secrets they held. Arthur's writing became more frantic and disjointed, with sketches of symbols and references to an "ancient curse."

Among the papers, she found a faded photograph of a young woman with hauntingly familiar features. The photo was labeled "Isabella Blackwood, 1894." Evelyn's heart skipped a beat. The name Blackwood had been prominent in Arthur's writings, and Isabella was a name she had encountered before. She recognized her striking resemblance to a portrait she had seen in the hallway.

The photograph stirred a memory of a local legend she had heard as a child — a tale of a woman who had disappeared under mysterious circumstances. Evelyn had dismissed it as folklore, but now it seemed more than just a story. The photograph suggested a deeper connection between Isabella's fate and the eerie events at the mansion.

As she continued her investigation, the storm outside showed no signs of letting up. The wind howled, and the rain beat against the windows with relentless force. The atmosphere in the manor grew heavier, as if the house itself was alive with ancient secrets.

She glanced at the clock — it was nearing 2 am. She knew she had to complete her assessment of the manor before morning, but the mounting sense of dread made it difficult to focus. Shadows seemed to dance at the edge of her vision, and every creak of the floorboards was magnified in the stillness of the night.

She decided to explore more of the mansion, hoping to find additional clues or answers to the strange occurrences. As she moved through the darkened halls, each creak of the floorboards and whisper of the wind seemed to heighten her anxiety. The portraits of the Blackwood family seemed to watch her as she passed, their eyes following her every movement.

The mansion seemed to hold its breath as Evelyn ventured further into its depths. The grandeur of the once-luxurious rooms was now marred by decay and neglect. She found herself in a grand ballroom, where the chandelier hung like a ghostly specter above. The once-vibrant tapestries were now faded and tattered, and the floor was covered in a thick layer of dust.

Her flashlight flickered, casting erratic shadows on the walls. She noticed a large, ornate mirror at one end of the ballroom. The mirror's surface was streaked with grime, but as she cleaned it, she noticed an inscription etched into the frame: "In shadows, truth awaits." Her fingers traced the letters, feeling a shiver run down her spine. The mirror's reflection seemed to twist with the storm's light, and for a brief moment, she thought she saw a figure standing behind her — a fleeting image that vanished as quickly as it had appeared.

Determined to find answers, Evelyn returned to the study and continued her examination of the artifacts and documents. She discovered more about the Blackwood family's history — an intricate tapestry of wealth, tragedy, and mystery. Each discovery deepened the enigma surrounding the mansion and its ghostly inhabitants.

As the first light of dawn began to seep through the storm clouds, Evelyn finally felt a sense of relief. The storm had subsided, and the mansion, though still shrouded in its eerie aura, seemed less oppressive. The haunting of the night had left its mark, but Evelyn was resolute in her quest for the truth.

She took one last look around the study, feeling a mixture of apprehension and determination. The mysterious inheritance had brought her face-to-face with something far beyond her expectations, and she was resolute in uncovering the truth about Blackwood Hall. With a heavy heart but a renewed sense of purpose, she prepared to spend the day cataloging the manor's contents and planning her next steps. The ghostly encounter and the secrets of the Blackwood family were just the beginning of a journey that promised to be both thrilling and terrifying.

Chapter 2

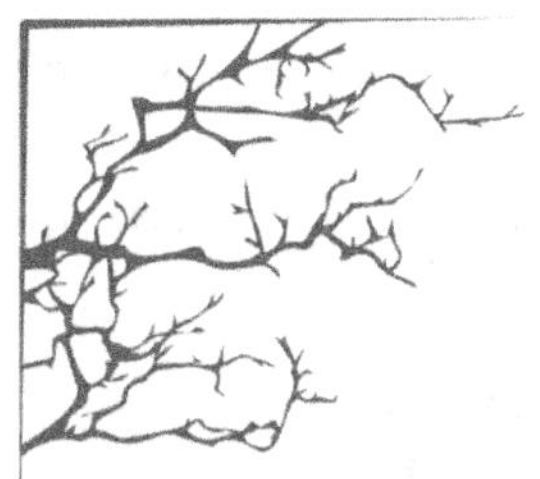

The morning sun struggled to pierce through the heavy storm clouds, casting a pale light over Blackwood Hall. Evelyn woke up to the remnants of the storm, the once-violent winds now reduced to a gentle breeze. The mansion, still cloaked in an eerie silence, seemed to be recovering from the tempest that had rattled its very bones.

She had managed to get some rest, though her sleep was fitful and haunted by dreams of shadowy figures and cryptic messages. As she moved through the manor, she could still feel the lingering tension from the previous night. The mansion's oppressive atmosphere weighed heavily on her, but she was determined to uncover the truth.

She decided to start her day by exploring more of the mansion. She made her way through the grand hallways, now illuminated by the soft morning light. The once-majestic walls were lined with faded portraits and intricate tapestries, each telling a story of its own.

Her footsteps echoed as she walked through the dusty corridors, her flashlight now replaced by the weak sunlight filtering through the grimy windows. She stopped to examine the portraits, noting the stern faces of the Blackwood ancestors. The eyes of the figures seemed to follow her, adding to the unsettling ambiance of the mansion.

Her first destination was the mansion's library, a room she had yet to explore. The library was a large, dimly lit space filled with rows of towering bookshelves. The air was thick with the smell of old books and leather. Dust particles floated lazily in the sunlight, creating an almost magical atmosphere.

As she began to sift through the books and documents, she noticed a collection of old ledgers and journals tucked away in a corner. These seemed to be more personal in nature compared to the academic works she had seen in the study. She picked up a leather-bound journal and opened it, discovering it was a personal diary belonging to Isabella Blackwood.

The diary was filled with eloquent entries, detailing Isabella's daily life and her feelings of isolation. Evelyn read passages about Isabella's struggles with the mansion's oppressive atmosphere and her growing sense of dread. The diary hinted at a dark presence in the house that had begun to torment Isabella, echoing some of the experiences Evelyn had felt the previous night.

One entry in particular caught her eye:

"I can no longer tell where my thoughts end and the whispers of the house begin. It feels as though the walls themselves are alive, watching me with hidden eyes."

The entry was dated just before Isabella's disappearance, adding to the sense of mystery surrounding her fate. Evelyn felt a chill run down her spine as she realized that Isabella's experiences were eerily similar to her own.

As she continued her research in the library, the sound of footsteps approached from the hallway. She looked up, expecting to see a member of the household staff, but instead found herself face-to-face with an elderly woman. The woman was dressed in old-fashioned clothing, her appearance strikingly out of place in the modern world.

"Good morning," Evelyn said, trying to mask her surprise. "Can I help you?"

The woman introduced herself as Mrs. Hawthorne, the last remaining servant of the Blackwood estate. She had come to offer her assistance, having heard about Evelyn's arrival from a neighbor. Mrs. Hawthorne's eyes were kind but held a glimmer of sadness as she spoke.

"The manor has been quiet for so long," Mrs. Hawthorne said, her voice tinged with nostalgia. "It's rare for someone to come back here, especially someone who doesn't know the stories."

Mrs. Hawthorne began to share her memories of the Blackwood family, recounting tales of the mansion's history and its former inhabitants. She spoke of Arthur's obsession with the supernatural and the strange events that had occurred before his death. According to her, many of the staff had left the manor due to the growing rumors of hauntings and curses.

One particular story caught Evelyn's attention. Mrs. Hawthorne mentioned a hidden room in the mansion that was rumored to hold secrets about the Blackwood family's past. She described it as being concealed behind a false wall in one of the upper floors.

Evelyn listened intently, her curiosity piqued. The idea of a hidden room aligned with some of the clues she had uncovered, including the mysterious symbols and references in Arthur's journal.

Determined to investigate, Evelyn thanked Mrs. Hawthorne and set out to find the hidden room. She climbed the creaking staircase to the upper floors, her flashlight casting long shadows on the walls. Each step felt like a journey deeper into the mansion's secrets.

After searching through various rooms, she found what she was looking for. In an old bedroom, she noticed a section of the wall that seemed slightly different from the rest. The wallpaper was more faded, and the woodwork appeared slightly disjointed.

Using a tool she found in the study, she pried open the panel, revealing a hidden compartment. Inside, she discovered an old chest covered in dust. With a deep breath, she opened the chest, finding it filled with more letters, photographs, and old family records.

Among the items was a letter, addressed to Arthur from an unknown sender. The letter was written in a formal, almost archaic style and contained a cryptic message:

"The past cannot be undone, and the shadows you seek are but reflections of the truth you have yet to uncover. Beware the echoes of the forgotten, for they hold the keys to your fate."

The letter's ominous tone sent a shiver down Evelyn's spine. She felt that it was a direct warning about the dangers she might face as she delved deeper into the mansion's history.

As she examined the contents of the chest, she stumbled upon a small, intricately carved wooden box. Inside, she found a locket with a portrait of a woman who looked strikingly similar to Isabella Blackwood. The locket was engraved with the initials "I.B." and a date that matched the period of Isabella's disappearance.

The discovery of the locket raised more questions than answers. Why was it hidden in the chest, and what did it signify about Isabella's fate?

With the hidden room's secrets revealed, Evelyn felt a renewed sense of purpose. The locket, along with the other documents, suggested that there were deeper mysteries to uncover about the Blackwood family and the ghostly occurrences in the mansion.

As the day wore on, she prepared to explore the mansion further, driven by the revelations she had uncovered. The storm had passed, but the real tempest of Blackwood Hall's secrets was just beginning to unfold.

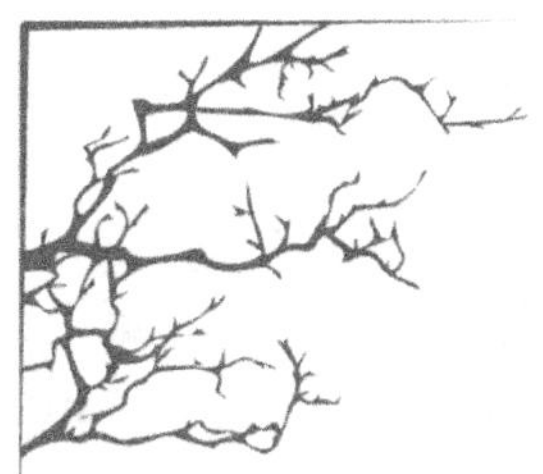

Chapter 3

The morning sun cast a muted light over Blackwood Hall as Evelyn continued her exploration of the mansion. With the storm's fury now a distant memory, the manor seemed almost serene, but its silence was unsettling. The discoveries from the previous day had only deepened the mystery, and Evelyn felt a growing sense of urgency.

She decided to spend the day examining the documents and artifacts she had uncovered. The letter and the locket hinted at deeper secrets within the mansion, and she was determined to piece together the puzzle. She set up a workspace in the library, spreading out the items she had found and organizing them for closer inspection.

The letter she had discovered in the hidden chest was particularly troubling. Its message, "The past cannot be undone, and the shadows you seek are but reflections of the truth you have yet to uncover," seemed to be a direct challenge. She wondered who had sent it and what "echoes of the forgotten" referred to.

As she examined the letter again, she noticed a subtle watermark on the paper — an emblem of a crest she had not seen before. The crest featured an ornate design with a central motif of an hourglass surrounded by vines. She made a note to research this symbol further, as it might provide clues to the sender's identity or intentions.

The locket with the portrait of Isabella Blackwood was another intriguing find. Evelyn carefully opened it again, studying the intricate details. The portrait showed a young woman with a melancholic expression, her eyes seeming to hold a story of their own. The initials "I.B." and the date on the locket suggested a personal connection to Isabella, but the exact significance remained unclear.

Evelyn decided to investigate the locket's origins. She used the library's resources to search for any historical records or references to the locket or similar jewelry. Her research led her to old family records and genealogies, but she found no direct mention of the locket.

While she was engrossed in her research, the library door creaked open. She looked up to see Mrs. Hawthorne standing in the doorway, holding a small tray with tea and biscuits. The elderly woman's kind eyes met Evelyn's with a mixture of curiosity and concern.

"I thought you might need a break," Mrs. Hawthorne said softly, placing the tray on a nearby table. "The manor can be quite overwhelming, especially for someone new."

Evelyn thanked her and invited her to join her. Over tea, Mrs. Hawthorne shared more about the Blackwood family's history, including stories of the manor's past inhabitants. She spoke of Isabella Blackwood with reverence, describing her as a beloved member of the family who had been deeply affected by the mansion's strange occurrences.

She mentioned that Isabella had been engaged to a man named Jonathan Blake, a local historian who had been interested in the Blackwood family's history. Jonathan had mysteriously disappeared shortly after Isabella's vanishing, and his disappearance was never solved. This connection intrigued Evelyn, as it suggested a possible link between Isabella's fate and the mysterious events surrounding the manor.

Mrs. Hawthorne also spoke of a family heirloom — a brooch that had belonged to Isabella. The brooch was said to be of great value and was rumored to have been hidden before her disappearance. Evelyn wondered if the brooch could be related to the locket and the secrets she was uncovering.

After Mrs. Hawthorne left, Evelyn resumed her investigation. Her attention turned to the upper floors of the mansion, where she had noticed a peculiar staircase in one of the old photographs she had found. The photograph showed a hidden staircase that seemed to lead to a part of the manor not accessible from the current layout.

Determined to find out more, Evelyn explored the upper floors, searching for any signs of a concealed staircase. Her efforts led her to a dusty, unused hallway that had been sealed off. With some effort, she managed to pry open the door and found a narrow staircase leading downward.

The air was musty and cool as she descended the stairs, her flashlight illuminating the dark, winding passage. The staircase ended at a small, dimly lit room filled with old furniture and cobwebs. In the center of the room was a large wooden chest, similar to the one she had found in the hidden room.

She approached the chest with a mixture of excitement and trepidation. She opened it carefully, revealing an assortment of old documents, letters, and personal items. Among them was another journal, this one belonging to Jonathan Blake. The journal was filled with notes on the Blackwood family's history and mentions of a secret that had been hidden for generations.

One entry caught Evelyn's eye:

"The Blackwood curse is not merely a tale. There are deeper truths buried within these walls, waiting to be revealed. The brooch holds the key to understanding the curse and the fate of Isabella."

The mention of the brooch confirmed Evelyn's suspicions and provided a new lead. The journal also included sketches of the brooch and descriptions of its intricate design. Evelyn recognized the design from the family records she had reviewed earlier.

With the discovery of Jonathan Blake's journal, Evelyn felt both elation and apprehension. The pieces of the puzzle were starting to come together, but the more she uncovered, the more complex the mystery became. The connection between Isabella's disappearance, Jonathan's research, and the cursed brooch added layers to the enigma of Blackwood Hall.

As evening approached, Evelyn resolved to continue her investigation into the brooch and its connection to the mansion's dark history. The hidden staircase and the chest had revealed new clues, but they also raised more questions. What secrets did the brooch hold? How were the various elements of the curse connected?

Evelyn knew that the answers were hidden somewhere within the mansion's walls, and she was determined to find them. The echoes of the past were growing louder, and the truth was just beyond her grasp.

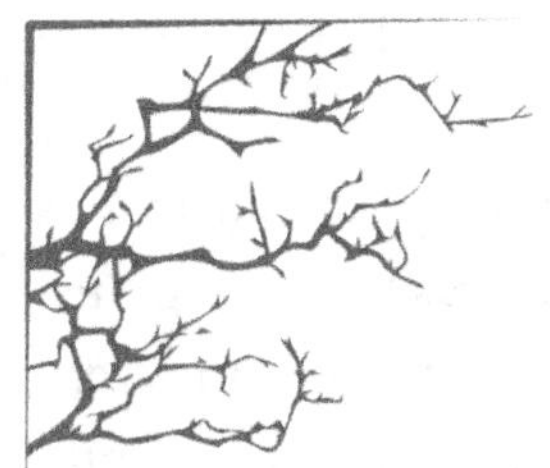

Chapter 4

The following day at Blackwood Hall was overcast, with a thick blanket of clouds hiding the sun. The mansion's somber atmosphere seemed to reflect the mounting tension Evelyn felt as she delved deeper into the mysteries surrounding it. The discoveries she had made — Jonathan Blake's journal, the locket, and the cryptic letter — had intensified her determination to uncover the truth.

She awoke with a sense of urgency. She felt as though the mansion itself was holding its breath, waiting for her to uncover its secrets. Her immediate goal was to investigate the attic, a place she had yet to explore and which seemed to hold potential clues.

She started her day by revisiting the library to review Jonathan Blake's journal. The sketches and notes about the brooch and the curse led her to believe that the attic might contain more information about the Blackwood family's hidden history. She had noticed an old, dusty door on the upper floor that seemed to lead to the attic but had been too focused on other areas to explore it.

After gathering her flashlight and a few essential tools, she climbed the creaky stairs to the attic door. It was heavy and ornate, with intricate carvings that matched some of the designs she had seen in the mansion's other rooms. She took a deep breath and pushed the door open, revealing a dark and musty space.

The attic was a vast, cluttered area filled with old trunks, furniture, and stacks of newspapers. The air was thick with dust, and the sunlight streaming through the small, grimy window cast eerie shadows across the room. She carefully stepped over piles of debris, her flashlight cutting through the darkness.

As she sifted through the forgotten belongings, she noticed several old trunks and boxes stacked against one wall. They were covered in layers of dust, indicating that they hadn't been touched in years. With a sense of anticipation, she began to open them one by one.

The first trunk she opened was filled with old clothing and accessories from a bygone era. Among the items were a delicate lace dress and an antique jewelry box. She carefully examined the jewelry box, hoping to find something of significance. Inside, she found several pieces of ornate jewelry, including a brooch that matched the design described in Jonathan Blake's journal.

The brooch was intricately crafted, with a central gemstone surrounded by intricate filigree. Evelyn's heart raced as she realized the brooch might be the very item Jonathan had written about. She took note of its details and carefully placed it in her bag for further examination.

Moving on to the next trunk, she discovered a collection of old photographs and letters. The photographs showed various members of the Blackwood family, including some that matched the portraits she had seen in the manor. One photograph depicted a family gathering, with a younger Arthur Blackwood and Isabella in the center. Their expressions were solemn, hinting at the underlying tension that plagued the family.

The letters were addressed to various family members and included personal correspondence as well as business dealings. One letter, in particular, stood out. It was from Jonathan Blake, addressed to Arthur Blackwood, and contained a request for information about the family's history. The letter was polite but carried an undertone of urgency, indicating that Jonathan was seeking something crucial.

Evelyn's exploration led her to a small, ornate box hidden behind some old furniture. The box was locked, but she managed to pry it open with a tool she had brought. Inside, she found a collection of old documents, including a detailed family tree and several handwritten notes.

The family tree was annotated with various names and dates, showing the Blackwood lineage and its connections to other prominent families. Evelyn noticed several names marked with red ink, including Isabella and Jonathan. The annotations indicated a series of events and relationships that were not mentioned in the official family records.

The handwritten notes were even more intriguing. They described a secret society that was rumored to have existed within the Blackwood family. The notes mentioned rituals, hidden chambers, and a quest for a powerful artifact believed to be linked to the family's curse.

As Evelyn examined the documents, she noticed a reference to a hidden chamber within the mansion. The notes described a concealed room that could only be accessed through a specific mechanism in the attic. The description matched some of the architectural features she had observed earlier.

Determined to find the hidden chamber, Evelyn searched the attic for any clues that might reveal its location. After a thorough search, she found a small, inconspicuous lever hidden behind a stack of old crates. With a sense of anticipation, she pulled the lever, and a section of the wall creaked open, revealing a narrow passageway.

She squeezed through the passageway, which led her to a small, dimly lit room. The space was lined with shelves and cabinets, filled with dusty old books and artifacts. In the center of the room was a large, ornate chest, similar to the one she had found earlier.

The chest was adorned with intricate carvings and had a combination lock. She carefully examined the lock, noting the symbols and patterns engraved on it. The combination appeared to be related to the family's history and the curse described in Jonathan Blake's journal.

After some experimentation, she managed to open the chest. Inside, she found a collection of ancient manuscripts, maps, and a diary that belonged to Isabella Blackwood. The diary was filled with entries about the hidden chamber, the family's secrets, and the mysterious artifact that was said to be the key to breaking the curse.

The diary described the artifact as a powerful relic that had been hidden to protect it from those who sought to misuse its power. The artifact was believed to hold the key to the Blackwood family's curse, and the diary contained detailed instructions on how to find and use it.

Evelyn carefully read through the diary, noting the steps required to locate the artifact and the rituals associated with it. The instructions were complex and required a deep understanding of the family's history and the mansion's architecture.

With the discovery of the hidden chamber and the diary, Evelyn felt a renewed sense of purpose. The clues she had uncovered provided a clear path to uncovering the truth behind the Blackwood family's curse and the fate of Isabella Blackwood.

As she prepared to leave the attic, she realized that the mansion's secrets were more intertwined with her own investigation than she had initially thought. The echoes of the past were growing louder, and the answers she sought were hidden within the walls of Blackwood Hall.

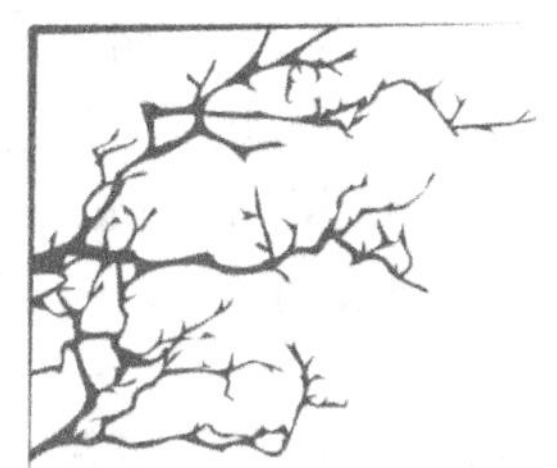

Chapter 5

As Evelyn descended from the attic, she felt a mixture of excitement and trepidation. The hidden chamber had revealed more than she had hoped for: Isabella Blackwood's diary and clues about a mysterious artifact linked to the Blackwood family curse. She knew that understanding these revelations was crucial to solving the mystery of the manor.

Back in the library, she carefully spread out the contents of the chest: the ancient manuscripts, maps, and Isabella's diary. She focused first on the diary, its pages yellowed with age and filled with Isabella's elegant handwriting. The diary detailed the artifact's significance and provided a series of instructions and warnings about its power.

Isabella wrote extensively about the artifact, describing it as a powerful object imbued with dark energy. According to the diary, the artifact had been hidden to protect it from those who would seek to exploit its power. The diary also mentioned a series of rituals required to find and access the artifact.

The diary included a map of the mansion's grounds, with specific markings indicating locations where clues to the artifact's whereabouts could be found. One location stood out: a hidden compartment within the old chapel on the estate grounds. The map showed a secret passage leading from the chapel to an underground chamber.

Evelyn decided to investigate the chapel. The weather outside was overcast, and a light drizzle began to fall, adding to the somber atmosphere. She gathered her flashlight and a few essential items, determined to follow the clues laid out in Isabella's diary.

The old chapel was located on the estate grounds, a short walk from the mansion. It was a gothic structure, with weathered stone walls and a tall, arched entrance. The chapel had been unused for many years, its doors and windows covered in grime and overgrowth.

Evelyn approached the chapel, her footsteps crunching on the gravel path. The building appeared forlorn, its once-grand architecture now faded and neglected. She carefully pushed open the heavy wooden doors, which creaked ominously.

Inside, the chapel was dimly lit by the weak daylight filtering through the stained glass windows. Particles of dust floated in the air, adding to the eerie ambiance. Evelyn's flashlight illuminated the interior, revealing worn pews and a dilapidated altar.

She began her search by examining the altar, noting its intricate carvings and faded inscriptions. She remembered the map's instructions, which indicated a hidden compartment beneath the altar. She carefully inspected the altar's base and discovered a small, nearly invisible latch.

With a sense of anticipation, she pulled the latch, and a section of the altar's base slid open, revealing a narrow passageway. She hesitated for a moment before entering, her flashlight illuminating the dark, musty space.

The passage led to an underground chamber that was surprisingly well-preserved. The chamber was circular, with stone walls and a vaulted ceiling. In the center of the room was a pedestal, upon which rested an ornate chest covered in dust.

Evelyn approached the chest, her heart racing. The chest was similar in design to the one she had found in the hidden room, but it was adorned with additional symbols and carvings. She carefully examined the chest, noting the intricate patterns that matched the symbols described in Isabella's diary.

The chest was locked with a combination mechanism, and Evelyn used the instructions from the diary to decipher the code. The symbols on the chest matched some of the symbols in the diary's illustrations. After aligning the symbols correctly, the chest creaked open, revealing its contents.

Inside the chest, she found a collection of old manuscripts, artifacts, and a small, intricately designed relic. The relic was a pendant with an unusual gemstone, set in an elaborate gold setting. The design of the pendant matched descriptions of the artifact in Isabella's diary.

She carefully examined the pendant, noting its craftsmanship and the aura of ancient power it seemed to radiate. The diary had warned that the relic was linked to the family's curse and could be dangerous if mishandled. Evelyn felt a chill as she considered the implications of her discovery.

As she examined the relic, she noticed that it was engraved with symbols that corresponded to the curse described in Jonathan Blake's journal. The relic appeared to be the key to understanding the curse and possibly breaking it.

While Evelyn was engrossed in her examination of the relic, she felt a sudden drop in temperature and a sense of being watched. The chapel's atmosphere grew heavy, and she heard a faint whispering sound, as though voices from the past were reaching out to her.

Her flashlight flickered, and the shadows in the chamber seemed to shift and writhe. She took a deep breath, trying to steady her nerves, and continued her examination of the relic. The whispers grew louder, and she could barely make out fragments of words — warnings and cries for help from the past.

The relic's inscriptions and the diary's instructions provided her with a clearer understanding of the curse. It was linked to a pact made by the Blackwood family ancestors, involving the relic and a dark ritual that had gone awry. The artifact was central to the curse's power and was believed to hold the key to both the curse and the family's salvation.

Evelyn knew that she needed to proceed with caution. The relic was a powerful and potentially dangerous object, and its role in the curse meant that uncovering the truth would not be easy.

As Evelyn left the underground chamber, she felt a renewed sense of purpose. The relic and the clues she had uncovered pointed to a complex and dangerous history, but they also offered hope for breaking the curse and uncovering the truth about the Blackwood family.

With the relic safely secured, Evelyn returned to the mansion, her mind racing with thoughts of the next steps in her investigation. The secrets of Blackwood Hall were becoming clearer, but the journey ahead promised to be fraught with challenges and dangers.

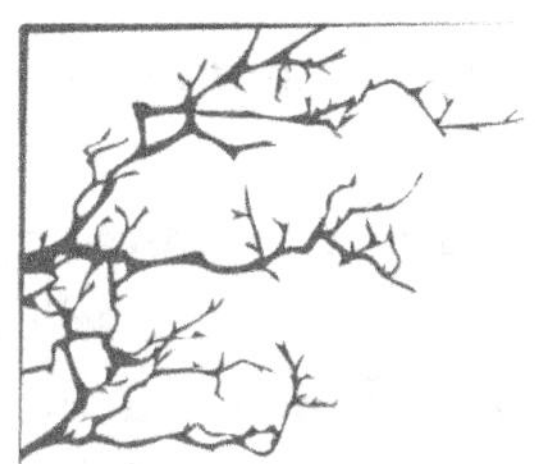

Chapter 6

Back at Blackwood Hall, Evelyn felt a mix of excitement and trepidation. The relic she had uncovered in the chapel was a significant find, but its implications were daunting. She knew that the artifact was central to the Blackwood family curse and might hold the key to unraveling the mystery surrounding Isabella Blackwood's disappearance and the manor's dark history.

Evelyn took the relic to her temporary study — a room she had set up for her research. The room was quiet and dimly lit, with the only illumination coming from a desk lamp and the flickering flames of a nearby fireplace. She carefully placed the pendant on the desk, examining it closely. Its intricate design and the symbols engraved on it seemed to pulse with an otherworldly energy.

To better understand the relic's significance, she began by comparing it to the notes and illustrations in Jonathan Blake's journal and Isabella's diary. The symbols on the pendant matched those described in the texts, suggesting that the artifact played a central role in the curse. She noticed that the gemstone in the pendant had an unusual, shifting color that seemed to reflect different shades depending on the light.

As she studied the relic, she recalled the cryptic warning from the letter she had found in the hidden chest: "The shadows you seek are but reflections of the truth you have yet to uncover."

She wondered if the pendant was connected to this warning and if it held secrets beyond its apparent design.

While deep in thought, she began to feel a strange sensation — an inexplicable chill that seemed to emanate from the relic itself. The room's temperature dropped, and shadows in the corners of the room seemed to flicker and shift. Evelyn's heart raced as she tried to shake off the eerie feeling.

Suddenly, the room was filled with a soft, ghostly glow. She looked up to see a translucent figure standing in the corner of the room. The apparition resembled a young woman, dressed in early 20th-century attire. Her face was partially obscured, but her eyes seemed to plead for help.

The ghostly figure spoke in a faint, echoing voice: "The truth lies buried in the shadows of the past. The relic holds the key. Find the hourglass."

Evelyn watched in shock as the apparition faded, leaving behind an unsettling silence. The vision had been brief but impactful, reinforcing the idea that the relic was indeed connected to a deeper mystery. She knew she needed to find out more about the hourglass mentioned by the ghost.

Determined to uncover the significance of the hourglass, Evelyn turned to the library's resources. She scoured through historical records, family documents, and old photographs, searching for any reference to an hourglass or related artifacts.

After several hours of research, she came across a mention of an hourglass in a family ledger from the early 1900s. The ledger described an ornate hourglass that had been a prized possession of the Blackwood family. It was said to have been displayed prominently in the manor's great hall before it mysteriously vanished.

Evelyn's curiosity was piqued. She wondered if the missing hourglass was connected to the relic and if its location might hold additional clues about the curse and Isabella's fate.

The great hall of Blackwood Hall was an expansive and imposing space. It featured high ceilings, grand chandeliers, and large, intricately carved fireplaces. The hall had been largely untouched since the manor's abandonment, with dust covering the furniture and cobwebs hanging from the corners.

Evelyn decided to investigate the great hall, focusing on areas where the hourglass might have been displayed. She carefully examined the walls and the fireplace, looking for any signs of concealed compartments or hidden storage.

As she inspected the room, she came across an ornate wooden cabinet that had been partially hidden behind a large draped curtain. The cabinet was intricately carved and appeared to be an antique. She noticed that it had a keyhole, but the cabinet was locked.

She searched the great hall for a key that might fit the cabinet. She recalled that some of the trunks and boxes she had previously found in the attic contained old keys and trinkets. She returned to her study and sifted through the old boxes, hoping to find a key that might match.

After some searching, she discovered an old, ornate key that seemed to fit the description of the keyhole in the cabinet. She returned to the great hall and carefully inserted the key into the lock. With a click, the cabinet door swung open.

Inside the cabinet, Evelyn found a collection of old, dusty items, including several framed portraits, a set of antique candlesticks, and a large, covered object. She carefully removed the cover to reveal a beautiful, ornate hourglass. Its base was intricately carved, and the glass was filled with fine, golden sand.

The hourglass matched the description from the ledger and appeared to be in excellent condition. She felt a sense of triumph as she realized that this might be the missing piece to solving the mystery.

As she examined the hourglass, she noted that it was inscribed with symbols similar to those on the pendant. The hourglass seemed to radiate a faint glow, and the sand inside appeared to flow in a slow, mesmerizing pattern. Evelyn wondered if the hourglass played a role in the rituals described in the diary and if it was connected to the curse.

She carefully transported it back to her study, setting it alongside the relic. The two items seemed to complement each other, and Evelyn felt that she was on the brink of a major breakthrough.

As she continued her research, she came across a passage in Isabella's diary that mentioned the hourglass as a key component of the family's rituals. The diary described how the hourglass was used to mark significant moments and to channel the energy required for the ritual. The relic and the hourglass were believed to be interconnected, and understanding their relationship was crucial to breaking the curse.

She knew that the next step in her investigation would be to perform the ritual described in the diary. The ritual was complex and required specific conditions, including the alignment of the hourglass and the relic. Evelyn felt both excitement and apprehension as she prepared to undertake this task.

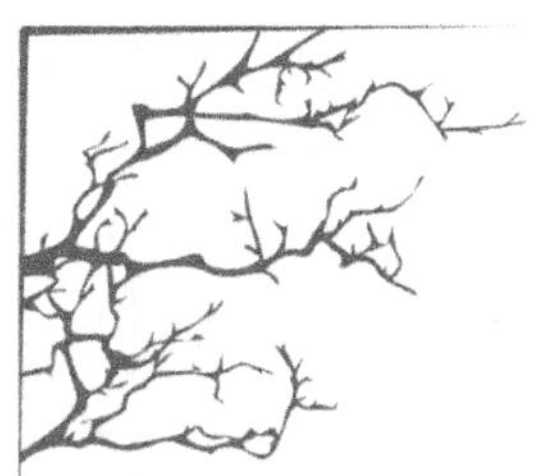

Chapter 7

With the hourglass and the relic now in her possession, Evelyn felt a renewed sense of urgency. The discoveries she had made — the hourglass, the relic, and the cryptic clues — had pointed her towards an ancient ritual that might hold the key to unraveling the curse afflicting Blackwood Hall. She had studied the instructions in Isabella Blackwood's diary thoroughly and understood that performing the ritual required precise preparation and timing.

The ritual described in the diary was intricate and demanded specific conditions to be met. Evelyn carefully reviewed the diary's notes, which included detailed instructions about the ritual's requirements: the positioning of the hourglass and the relic, the recitation of ancient incantations, and the alignment of certain symbols.

She decided to perform the ritual in the grand ballroom of Blackwood Hall. The ballroom was a vast, elegant space with high ceilings, ornate chandeliers, and large windows that overlooked the estate's grounds. The room had been neglected for years, but its grandeur made it an ideal setting for the ritual.

She spent the afternoon preparing the ballroom. She cleared a central area for the ritual, placing the hourglass and the relic on a pedestal in the center of the room. She carefully arranged the items according to the instructions in the diary. The hourglass was positioned to the north, while the relic was placed to the south. She drew symbols on the floor using chalk, creating a pattern that matched the designs in the diary.

In addition to the hourglass and the relic, the ritual required several other components, including candles, incense, and specific herbs. Evelyn had gathered these items from various sources, including old supply rooms in the mansion and local shops. She arranged the candles around the ritual space, lighting them to create an aura of solemnity and focus.

She also prepared a small cauldron with a mixture of herbs and incense, as detailed in the diary. The fragrant smoke from the incense filled the ballroom, adding to the atmosphere of mystery and anticipation.

As night fell, Evelyn prepared herself mentally and emotionally for the ritual. She knew that performing it required complete concentration and adherence to the instructions. She took a deep breath, steadying herself, and began the ritual.

She recited the ancient incantations from Isabella's diary, her voice steady but filled with reverence. The words seemed to resonate with the room, and she felt a noticeable shift in the air. The hourglass began to glow faintly, and the sand inside flowed with an almost hypnotic rhythm.

As Evelyn continued the incantations, she noticed that the relic began to react. The gemstone in the pendant shimmered and changed colors, casting an ethereal light across the room. The symbols drawn on the floor seemed to come alive, glowing softly and casting intricate patterns on the walls.

She felt a surge of energy as the relic and the hourglass interacted. The room grew colder, and the shadows seemed to deepen. The whispers from earlier returned, more distinct and urgent. She strained to listen, trying to discern their meaning amidst the ritual's intensity.

As the ritual reached its climax, the ghostly figure Evelyn had seen before appeared once again. The apparition materialized in the center of the room, her expression more defined and her presence more intense. She appeared to be trying to communicate something crucial.

The apparition's voice was clearer now, though still faint: "The curse binds the souls to the manor. The hourglass marks the time. The truth is revealed when the final sands fall."

Evelyn listened intently, realizing that the ghost was providing a crucial piece of information. The hourglass was not only a symbol but also a key to understanding the timing and nature of the curse. The final sands falling might signify a pivotal moment in breaking the curse or revealing hidden truths.

Just as she began to grasp the significance of the apparition's message, a sudden gust of wind swept through the ballroom, extinguishing the candles and disrupting the ritual. The room was plunged into darkness, and the ambient temperature dropped drastically. Evelyn felt a surge of fear but remained determined.

The relic and the hourglass ceased their glow, and the symbols on the floor dimmed. The whispers grew louder, and Evelyn could hear the echoes of distant, anguished cries. She struggled to maintain her composure, knowing that the ritual's disruption might have unforeseen consequences.

She quickly relit the candles and attempted to restore the ritual's conditions. She recited the incantations again, focusing on recapturing the energy and alignment of the hourglass and the relic. The room slowly began to warm, and the shadows receded.

Despite her efforts, Evelyn sensed that the disruption had caused a shift in the ritual's progress. The apparition had vanished, leaving behind a lingering sense of urgency. She knew that she needed to revisit the diary and reassess her approach to fully understand the implications of the hourglass and the relic.

As she concluded the ritual, she noticed a faint, new inscription on the floor where the symbols had been drawn. It appeared to be a message, partially revealed by the shifting shadows. The inscription was written in an unfamiliar script, but Evelyn could make out a few key words: "Reveal," "Path," and "Legacy."

The new inscription seemed to indicate a path or location that might hold further clues about the curse and the Blackwood family's legacy. Evelyn felt a renewed sense of determination. The disruption had not deterred her but had instead provided a new lead.

She spent the remainder of the night reflecting on the ritual and the new information she had uncovered. She knew that the path ahead would be challenging and required careful consideration of the clues and messages she had received.

As she prepared for the next phase of her investigation, she was more resolute than ever. The mansion's secrets were beginning to unravel, and she was determined to uncover the truth behind the curse and the fate of the Blackwood family.

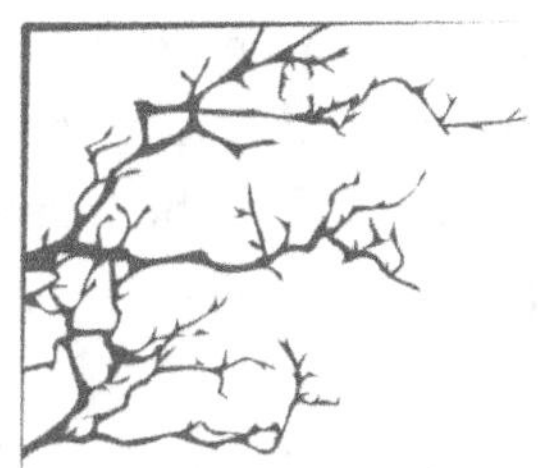

Chapter 8

With the ritual disrupted and the ballroom's atmosphere restored, Evelyn felt a mixture of frustration and resolve. The new inscription she had found on the floor, along with the ghostly apparition's message, hinted at further mysteries waiting to be uncovered. The words "Reveal," "Path," and "Legacy" suggested that there was more to discover about the Blackwood family's past and the curse afflicting the manor.

She spent the following morning analyzing the new inscription and cross-referencing it with the diary and other documents she had collected. The unfamiliar script on the floor appeared to be a variation of the symbols used in the ritual, but its full meaning remained unclear.

Realizing the complexity of the symbols and the potential importance of the new lead, she decided to seek external help. She contacted Dr. Clara Monroe, an expert in historical symbols and ancient scripts, who had previously assisted her with the diary. Dr. Monroe agreed to visit Blackwood Hall to provide insight into the new inscription.

She arrived in the early afternoon, bringing with her a range of reference materials and tools for analysis. Evelyn greeted her at the mansion's entrance and led her to the ballroom, where the new inscription was located.

In the grand ballroom, Dr. Monroe carefully examined the inscription on the floor. The script was intricate and resembled a combination of various ancient writing systems. With the help of her reference materials, Dr. Monroe began the process of deciphering the message.

Evelyn observed as Dr. Monroe worked, providing her with relevant context from the diary and the relic. The expert's focused attention and scholarly approach gave Evelyn hope that they would uncover the message's true meaning.

After several hours of intense analysis, Dr. Monroe made a breakthrough. She translated the inscription as follows: "In the chamber where shadows fall, seek the legacy of the fallen. The path lies where light and dark converge."

The translation suggested that there was a hidden chamber or location within the manor that held important clues about the Blackwood family's legacy. The reference to "shadows" and the convergence of "light and dark" indicated that the search would involve both physical and symbolic elements.

Evelyn and Dr. Monroe discussed possible locations within the manor that might fit the description. They considered areas such as hidden rooms, forgotten passages, and locations associated with past events in the Blackwood family's history.

Evelyn decided to focus on the manor's old servant quarters, which had been left largely unexplored. The quarters were located in a separate wing of the mansion and had been used by staff members who had worked for the Blackwood family. The area had a history of being a place of secrets and hidden passages.

She and Dr. Monroe made their way to the servant quarters, carrying flashlights and other equipment. The quarters were dusty and filled with old furniture and personal belongings.

Evelyn felt a sense of unease as they entered the area, knowing that it held the potential for uncovering hidden truths.

As they explored the servant quarters, they came across a large, ornate wardrobe that seemed out of place. The wardrobe was old and intricately designed, but it appeared to be more than just a piece of furniture.

Dr. Monroe carefully inspected the wardrobe and noticed that one of its panels had a faint outline of symbols carved into the wood. The symbols matched those found on the relic and in the diary. Evelyn and Dr. Monroe worked together to open the wardrobe, revealing a hidden mechanism behind one of the panels.

With a click, the wardrobe's panel slid open, revealing a narrow, hidden passage. The passage was dimly lit and seemed to lead deeper into the manor's structure.

They ventured into the passage, their flashlights illuminating the dark, musty space. The passage was narrow and winding, with old wooden walls and low ceilings. The air was thick with dust, and the atmosphere was heavy with the weight of the manor's forgotten history.

As they followed the passage, they noticed that the walls were adorned with faded murals and symbols, depicting scenes from the Blackwood family's past. The murals showed images of rituals, family members, and scenes of both light and darkness.

The passage eventually led to a hidden chamber, concealed behind a heavy, old door. The chamber was small and dimly lit by a single, flickering torch mounted on the wall. In the center of the room was an altar, surrounded by ancient relics and artifacts.

They carefully examined the chamber, noting its significance and the relevance of the items present. The altar was adorned with symbols similar to those found on the relic and the hourglass. The chamber seemed to be a place of both historical and symbolic importance.

On the altar, Evelyn found a set of old documents and artifacts, including family records, letters, and a journal. The journal appeared to be a personal account written by a member of the Blackwood family, detailing the family's history and the origins of the curse.

Evelyn and Dr. Monroe pored over the documents, discovering crucial information about the Blackwood family's past. The documents revealed details about the curse's origins, the role of the hourglass, and the dark pact made by the family's ancestors.

The journal described how the Blackwood family had made a pact with dark forces to gain power and influence. The pact had involved a ritual using the relic and the hourglass. The ritual had gone wrong, leading to the family's downfall and the curse that plagued the manor.

The documents also mentioned a hidden legacy — a key to breaking the curse that had been concealed within the manor. Evelyn realized that the chamber they had discovered was a crucial part of uncovering the truth and finding a way to break the curse.

With the new information in hand, Evelyn and Dr. Monroe felt a renewed sense of purpose. They understood that they were approaching the final stages of their investigation and that uncovering the truth about the Blackwood family's curse required careful planning and preparation.

Evelyn knew that the next steps would involve performing another ritual, using the knowledge gained from the hidden chamber and the documents they had uncovered. The journey was far from over, but Evelyn was determined to see it through and bring resolution to the Blackwood family's haunting legacy.

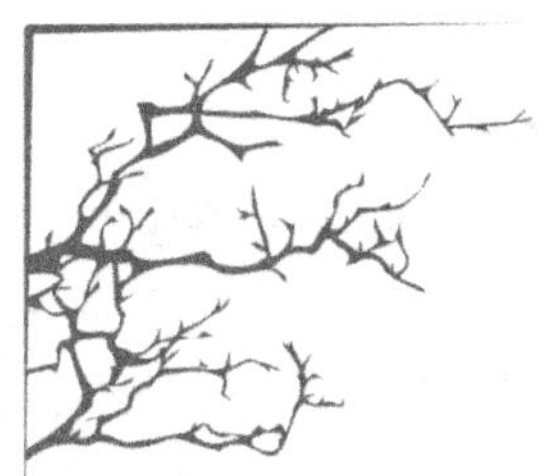

Chapter 9

With the discovery of the hidden chamber and the revelations from the journal, Evelyn was now on the cusp of a significant breakthrough in unraveling the curse of Blackwood Hall. She had gathered all the necessary components for the final ritual: the hourglass, the relic, and the newly discovered documents detailing the Blackwood family's dark past. The time had come to prepare for the final confrontation with the supernatural forces haunting the manor.

Evelyn spent the following days meticulously planning the ritual. The diary and the newly uncovered documents provided detailed instructions on how to perform the ritual to break the curse. The ritual involved aligning the hourglass and the relic in a specific manner, reciting ancient incantations, and performing a sequence of symbolic actions.

Evelyn chose the manor's old library as the location for the final ritual. The library was a large, atmospheric room filled with shelves of dusty books and faded tapestries. It had an air of mystery and history, making it an ideal setting for the culmination of her investigation.

She carefully prepared the room by clearing a central space and setting up the necessary items. The hourglass and the relic were placed on a grand, old wooden table at the center of the room. She drew symbols on the floor with chalk, creating a pattern that matched the instructions from the documents. She also set up candles and incense to create a solemn atmosphere.

In addition to the hourglass and the relic, the ritual required specific tools: a ceremonial dagger, a bowl of water, and a bundle of herbs. Evelyn had gathered these items from various sources, ensuring that each component was authentic and appropriate for the ritual.

The ceremonial dagger, an ornate piece with intricate engravings, was used in the ritual to symbolize the severing of ties with the curse. The bowl of water represented purification, and the herbs were used to create a protective barrier around the ritual space.

As night fell, Evelyn prepared herself mentally and emotionally for the ritual. She knew that this was the culmination of her investigation and that it required complete focus and adherence to the instructions. With everything in place, she began the ritual.

She recited the ancient incantations from the documents, her voice steady and clear. The words seemed to resonate with the room, and the atmosphere grew charged with energy. The hourglass began to glow softly, and the relic's gemstone shimmered with an ethereal light.

She performed the symbolic actions as described in the documents. She used the ceremonial dagger to draw a protective circle around the ritual space and then placed the dagger on the table. The bowl of water was placed next to the hourglass, and the herbs were arranged in a specific pattern around the room.

As Evelyn continued the ritual, the temperature in the room dropped, and a ghostly presence filled the library. The apparition of Isabella Blackwood appeared once again, her expression more intense and urgent. She watched as Evelyn performed the ritual, her gaze filled with both hope and desperation.

The apparition's voice echoed through the room: "The curse is bound by the legacy of the past. The final act must be completed to set the souls free."

Evelyn understood that the apparition's message was crucial to completing the ritual. The final act involved a key action or gesture that would break the curse and release the trapped souls.

As Evelyn neared the end of the ritual, she felt a powerful surge of energy. The hourglass's sand began to flow more rapidly, and the relic's light grew brighter. The room was filled with an intense, pulsating energy that seemed to resonate with the very walls of the manor.

The shadows in the room deepened and shifted, and Evelyn felt a profound sense of connection to the manor's history and the spirits trapped within. The ritual was reaching its climax, and the final gesture needed to be precise.

The final act of the ritual required Evelyn to use the ceremonial dagger to cut through the air above the hourglass, symbolizing the severing of the curse's hold. She raised the dagger and performed the gesture with careful precision, her focus unwavering.

As she completed the gesture, a blinding flash of light filled the room, and a powerful force seemed to emanate from the hourglass and the relic. The shadows and spirits in the room swirled and dissipated, and the oppressive atmosphere lifted.

The blinding light gradually faded, revealing a transformed library. The room felt lighter, and the oppressive presence that had lingered was gone. The hourglass and the relic ceased their glowing, and the symbols on the floor slowly faded away.

Evelyn looked around the library, feeling a sense of relief and accomplishment. The curse had been broken, and the manor was no longer haunted by the malevolent forces that had plagued it for so long.

Evelyn took a moment to reflect on her journey. The investigation had been challenging and fraught with danger, but the discoveries and the final ritual had brought resolution to the Blackwood family's haunting legacy. The spirits that had been trapped were now at peace, and the manor could finally be freed from its dark past.

As she stood in the library, she felt a sense of closure. The Blackwood family's story had been uncovered, and the curse had been lifted. She knew that the manor's history would continue to be a part of her, but she was ready to move forward.

With the curse lifted and the manor's dark history resolved, Evelyn prepared to leave Blackwood Hall. She knew that her work had made a significant impact, and she was grateful for the support of those who had helped her along the way.

She took one last look at the library and the manor, feeling a sense of accomplishment and hope. The journey had been long and arduous, but it had led to a resolution that would bring peace to the Blackwood family's legacy and to the manor itself.

As she departed, Evelyn knew that her work was far from over. The mysteries she had uncovered and the experiences she had gained would continue to guide her in future endeavors. The story of Blackwood Hall had come to an end, but her journey was just beginning.

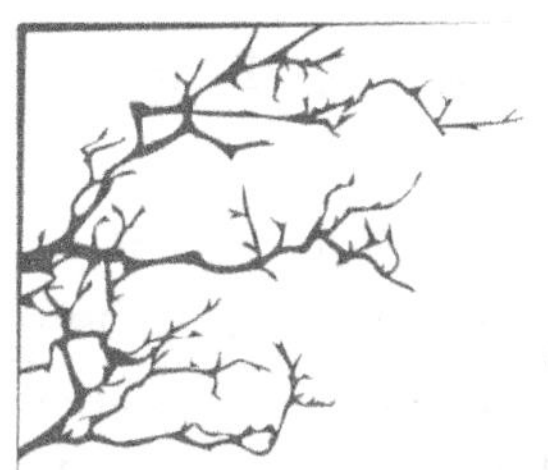

Chapter 10

With the curse lifted and the oppressive atmosphere that had haunted Blackwood Hall dissipated, Evelyn felt a profound sense of relief and accomplishment. The final ritual had been successfully completed, and the malevolent forces that had plagued the mansion for so long were no longer a threat. The manor, once shrouded in darkness and mystery, now seemed to breathe with a newfound sense of peace.

Evelyn spent the following days documenting the results of her investigation and the impact of the ritual. She meticulously recorded her findings and observations, noting the changes in the manor's atmosphere and the absence of the supernatural disturbances that had previously plagued her.

As she reviewed her notes and the journal of Isabella Blackwood, she reflected on the journey that had brought her to this point. The investigation had been challenging and emotionally taxing, but it had also been enlightening. She had uncovered the truth about the Blackwood family's curse and resolved the mystery that had haunted the manor for generations.

The diary had revealed the complexities of the curse and the historical context behind the Blackwood family's actions. Evelyn felt a deep sense of empathy for the spirits that had been trapped by the curse and was grateful for the opportunity to help them find peace.

Dr. Clara Monroe, who had been instrumental in deciphering the inscription and providing expertise throughout the investigation, visited Blackwood Hall to discuss the findings. Evelyn welcomed her with gratitude and shared the results of the final ritual.

Dr. Monroe expressed her admiration for Evelyn's work and the successful resolution of the curse. She also shared her own reflections on the investigation, noting the significance of the Blackwood family's legacy and the impact of the ritual on the manor's history.

During her final examination of the manor, Evelyn discovered a hidden compartment within the library's grand table. The compartment contained additional artifacts and documents related to the Blackwood family's history. These items included personal letters, family portraits, and a collection of rare books.

Among the documents, she found a letter addressed to her from Isabella Blackwood. The letter expressed gratitude for her efforts in breaking the curse and provided insights into the family's intentions and regrets. It also included a message of hope for future generations and a plea for forgiveness.

With the curse lifted, Evelyn worked with local historians and preservationists to restore Blackwood Hall to its former glory. The restoration process involved repairing the damage caused by years of neglect and ensuring that the manor's historical integrity was maintained.

The restoration efforts also included creating a museum space within the manor to showcase its history and the story of the Blackwood family. The museum would serve as a testament to the manor's rich heritage and the resolution of its dark past.

As the restoration progressed, Evelyn began to receive interest from historians, researchers, and visitors eager to learn about the manor's history and the investigation that had resolved its mysteries. The story of Blackwood Hall and its curse became a compelling tale of perseverance and redemption.

Evelyn's work had not only lifted the curse but had also brought new life to the manor and its history. The manor's legacy was now one of resolution and hope, rather than darkness and despair.

With the manor restored and the curse resolved, Evelyn prepared to move on to her next adventure. Her work at Blackwood Hall had been a profound experience, and she was eager to apply the lessons she had learned to future investigations.

Before leaving, she took one last tour of the manor, reflecting on the journey and the changes it had undergone. She felt a sense of satisfaction knowing that she had made a difference and had brought peace to a troubled place.

As she left Blackwood Hall, Evelyn looked back with a sense of accomplishment and gratitude. The manor's story had come full circle, and she was ready to embark on new challenges and discoveries.

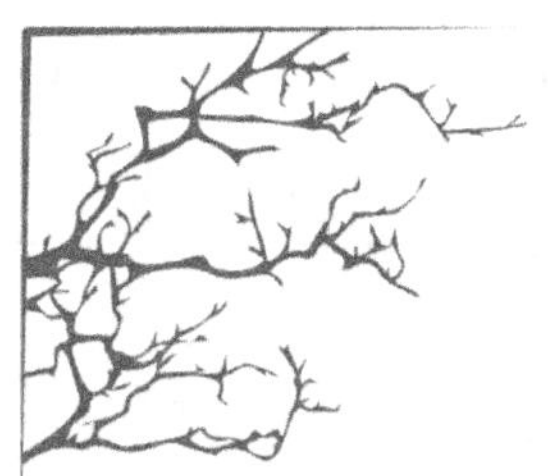

Chapter 11

After leaving Blackwood Hall and settling into her new routine, Evelyn Harper thought her involvement with the manor's mysteries was over. However, her work had left her with an enduring curiosity and a sense of unfinished business. One day, as she reviewed her notes and documents from the investigation, she came across a peculiar letter she had missed during her initial examination of the manor.

The letter was addressed to her from a local historian named Robert Sinclair, who had been researching the Blackwood family's history for years. Sinclair's letter contained a cryptic message about a hidden legacy connected to the manor that had not been fully uncovered.

Intrigued by the letter, she contacted him to learn more about his findings. Sinclair explained that he had uncovered references to a hidden legacy tied to the Blackwood family, which he believed could be crucial in understanding the full extent of the family's history and the curse.

According to Sinclair, there were additional documents and artifacts related to the Blackwood family that had been concealed from public view. These items were rumored to be hidden within a secret location on the manor's grounds, known only to a select few.

Evelyn decided to return to Blackwood Hall to investigate Sinclair's claims further. She arranged a meeting with him to discuss the details of his research and to plan their search for the hidden legacy.

Upon arriving at the manor, Evelyn was struck by how different it looked now that the curse had been lifted. The restoration work was nearly complete, and the manor's atmosphere had shifted from one of foreboding to one of calm and history.

Evelyn and Robert Sinclair began their search for the hidden legacy, focusing on areas of the manor that had not been thoroughly explored during the previous investigation. They examined old maps, architectural plans, and historical records to identify potential locations for the concealed items.

Their search led them to the manor's extensive grounds, including the overgrown gardens, forgotten outbuildings, and hidden compartments within the mansion itself. They also consulted with local historians and experts who had knowledge of the manor's history.

During their search, they uncovered several hidden clues that pointed them toward a concealed chamber beneath the manor's garden. The clues included symbols and markings that matched those found in the Blackwood family's documents.

After extensive investigation, they located a hidden entrance to an underground chamber buried beneath the garden. The entrance was concealed by overgrown vegetation and a layer of old stonework.

They descended into the underground chamber, their flashlights illuminating the dark, musty space. The chamber was surprisingly well-preserved and contained several artifacts and documents related to the Blackwood family.

Among the items they discovered were a series of letters, diaries, and personal belongings of the Blackwood family members. The documents revealed additional details about the family's history, including their connections to other influential families and their involvement in secret societies.

One of the most significant discoveries was a hidden journal belonging to Isabella Blackwood's ancestor, a powerful figure who had played a crucial role in the family's history. The journal detailed the origins of the Blackwood family's wealth and influence, as well as their involvement in occult practices and rituals.

The journal also contained information about a hidden legacy that had been passed down through generations. This legacy involved a series of ancient relics and documents that held the key to understanding the family's true power and influence.

Evelyn and Sinclair carefully studied the hidden journal and the associated artifacts. They learned that the Blackwood family's influence extended beyond the manor and involved a network of powerful individuals and secret societies. The hidden legacy revealed a deeper connection between the family's actions and the broader historical context of their time.

The documents also provided insight into the family's motivations and the reasons behind their involvement in dark practices. It became clear that the curse was a result of a complex web of power struggles, betrayals, and attempts to control forces beyond their understanding.

With the hidden legacy uncovered, Evelyn and Sinclair prepared to share their findings with the broader historical community. They planned to publish their research and present their discoveries in a series of lectures and articles.

Evelyn also considered the implications of the hidden legacy for her own future investigations. The revelations about the Blackwood family had opened new avenues for research and exploration, and she was eager to continue delving into the mysteries of history.

As she prepared to leave Blackwood Manor once again, she felt a renewed sense of purpose. The hidden legacy had provided valuable insights into the Blackwood family's history and had revealed new opportunities for exploration and discovery.

She bid farewell to Robert Sinclair and the restored manor, knowing that her journey had led her to a deeper understanding of the past. She was excited to embark on new adventures and continue uncovering the mysteries of history.

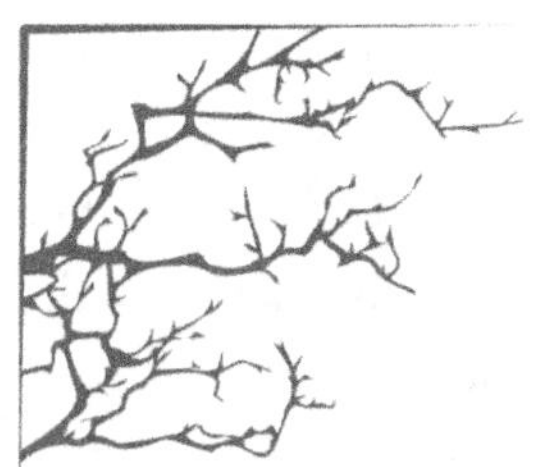

Chapter 12

After her return from Blackwood Manor and the discovery of the hidden legacy, Evelyn Harper found herself drawn back into the world of historical mysteries. The revelations about the Blackwood family had sparked her curiosity, and she was eager to explore further into the connections between the family's occult practices and their broader influence on history.

She received an invitation from an academic conference dedicated to occult history and historical mysteries. The conference was set to be held in a historic city known for its connections to secret societies and ancient practices. Evelyn saw this as an opportunity to present her findings and delve deeper into the connections between the Blackwood legacy and other historical phenomena.

She meticulously prepared her presentation, summarizing the discoveries about the Blackwood family's hidden legacy, their occult practices, and the implications of their influence on historical events. She gathered her research notes, prepared visual aids, and rehearsed her speech to ensure that her presentation would be both engaging and informative.

As the conference approached, she also took time to review the new documents and artifacts she had uncovered. She sought to draw connections between the Blackwood family's legacy and other historical figures and events related to the occult.

Upon arriving at the conference, she was impressed by the grandeur of the historic venue — a grand hall with intricate architecture and a rich history of its own. The conference attracted scholars, historians, and enthusiasts from around the world, all eager to explore the mysteries of the past.

Evelyn's presentation was met with great interest. She discussed the Blackwood family's history, their occult practices, and the hidden legacy she had uncovered. Her detailed research and compelling narrative captivated the audience, and she received positive feedback and questions from fellow scholars.

During the conference, she encountered a mysterious scholar named Dr. Adrian Blackwood, who claimed to be a distant relative of the Blackwood family. He was a tall, enigmatic figure with a deep knowledge of the occult and a keen interest in Evelyn's research.

He expressed a particular interest in the hidden journal and the relics she had discovered. He revealed that he had been researching the Blackwood family's occult practices for years and believed that there were even deeper secrets connected to the family's legacy.

He extended an invitation to Evelyn to visit his private study, where he claimed to have additional documents and artifacts related to the Blackwood family's occult practices. Intrigued by the offer and curious about the potential connections, she agreed to visit his study.

It was located in a historic mansion on the outskirts of the city. It was an opulent and foreboding space, filled with ancient books, occult symbols, and artifacts. Dr. Blackwood welcomed Evelyn and guided her through his collection, which included rare manuscripts and relics related to the Blackwood family and their occult practices.

As Evelyn examined Dr. Blackwood's collection, she uncovered new information that shed light on the Blackwood family's influence on occult practices and secret societies. Dr. Blackwood shared his theories about the family's role in shaping historical events and their connections to other powerful families and organizations.

He revealed that the Blackwood family had been involved in a secret society known as the "Order of the Veil," which sought to control supernatural forces and gain access to hidden knowledge. The society's influence extended across Europe and the Americas, and its members had played a significant role in shaping historical events.

He provided Evelyn with a new lead — a set of coordinates and a cryptic message that hinted at the location of another hidden legacy connected to the Blackwood family. The coordinates pointed to a remote location in a distant country, and the message suggested that this legacy could hold the key to understanding the full extent of the family's influence and power.

She felt a sense of excitement and trepidation as she considered the implications of this new lead. The possibility of uncovering more secrets and exploring new historical connections was both thrilling and daunting.

She decided to pursue the lead and planned her journey to the remote location indicated by the coordinates. She made arrangements for travel and began preparing for the challenges she might encounter.

In the meantime, she kept in touch with Dr. Blackwood and continued to review the documents and artifacts from his collection. She was eager to learn more about the Order of the Veil and its connections to the Blackwood family.

As she prepared to embark on her new adventure, she reflected on the journey that had led her to this point. The investigation into the Blackwood family's curse and hidden legacy had been a profound experience, and the new lead promised to expand her understanding of the family's influence and the occult practices they had been involved in.

She was excited about the possibilities that lay ahead and was ready to face whatever challenges and discoveries awaited her in her quest for knowledge. With a renewed sense of purpose and determination, she set out on her journey, ready to uncover the echoes of eternity and explore the hidden depths of history.